KAI:
NINJA OF FIRE

By Greg Farshtey

SCHOLASTIC INC.
New York   Toronto   London   Auckland
Sydney   Mexico City   New Delhi   Hong Kong

ISBN 978-0-545-39822-0

12 11 10 9 8 7 6 5 4 3 2 1   11 12 13 14 15 16/0

Printed in the U.S.A.   40
First printing, August 2011

CONTENTS

FROM THE JOURNAL OF SENSEI WU....... 1

IN HIS FOOTSTEPS 9

THE VANISHED VILLAGERS............. 21

CHAPTER 1....................... 23
CHAPTER 2....................... 29
CHAPTER 3....................... 36
CHAPTER 4....................... 40
CHAPTER 5....................... 56
CHAPTER 6....................... 60
CHAPTER 7....................... 67
CHAPTER 8....................... 72

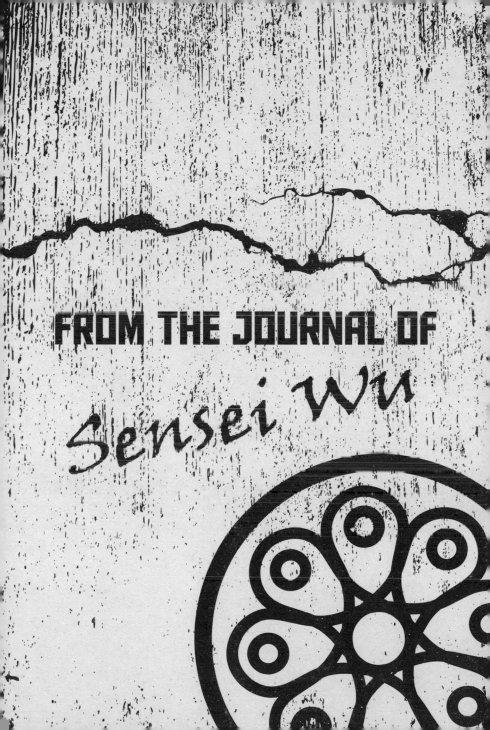

FROM THE JOURNAL OF

Sensei Wu

f the four young men I recruited to join my fight against Garmadon, easily the most . . . challenging was Kai. He was the last of the group and my hope was that he would become the Ninja of Fire. Certainly his temperament made him ideal for that element.

Kai is the son of one of my oldest and most trusted friends. He and his sister, Nya, were raised by their father. They lived in a little village, far from any major city, a place where one could work and strive for years and never be known outside the small

settlement. Kai's father worked as a black-smith and his apprentice was Kai.

Training Kai in the art of forging weapons and armor was, I gather, not an easy task, for the same reason it has not been easy to train him to be a ninja. He is impatient, reck-less, quick to anger, and reluctant to listen to the advice of others. His manner can be brash, but I believe that is a shield he has built against the world. With the passing of his father, Kai became the man of the family with the responsibility to look after his sister. That can be a great burden for a youth.

I found Kai and Nya at work in their shop, 4 Weapons. Unfortunately, Samukai and his skeleton warriors arrived at the same time, in search of a map that marked the locations of the Four Weapons of Spinjitzu. The skeletons attacked, and in the battle, made off with both the map and Nya. I convinced Kai that by accepting my training, he would have the best chance to retrieve his sister safely.

With the help of my other three young warriors, I set about teaching him what I could about the art of battle. It was not easy. The challenge was how to break him of his bad habits — rash actions, dangerous risk taking, and letting his emotions cloud his thoughts — without breaking his spirit. The other three, Cole, Jay, and Zane, had had more time together and knew how to work as a team. Kai was used to being on his own, except for Nya, and was reluctant to rely on others.

Ah, Nya . . . I do not know why Garmadon ordered the young girl's capture, except perhaps to use as a hostage against me in the future. Its most immediate effect was on Kai. He was consumed with the desire to rescue her, which blinded him to almost everything else. I feared that in the heat of battle he would put himself or the others in danger out of concern for Nya.

Still, there was much potential in Kai—
potential that I am happy to say was realized. He is brave, loyal, intelligent, and willing
to work hard to better himself. He has speed
and grace, two key ingredients in mastering
Spinjitzu. He is also fearless. I have no doubt
he would challenge Garmadon himself in single combat if given half a chance, and never
feel a moment's hesitation.

I look at Kai and I see his father. They share
the same tendency to rush headlong into danger, the same passion for life and devotion to
family, and even some of Kai's moves in mock
combat echo his father's. Kai did not know
of his father's past, thinking of him only as a
simple blacksmith, until I told him.

In the end, I am happy to say that Kai
justified my faith in him. He earned the Sword
of Fire he wields now. More important, he
learned to work as part of a team and to see
the grand picture of the world rather than

focusing on just his corner of it. He could have left with Nya and returned to his village and his old life, and no one would have thought less of him for it. But he chose to stand beside his partners and prepare for any future danger that might threaten.

Does he still leap into danger?

Yes. Is he still both amazing and exasperating? Yes. Is he like the fire he wields, burning hot and bright no matter what? Yes, indeed. He is Kai, unique as a spark of flame, sharp as the sword he carries, a true hero at last.

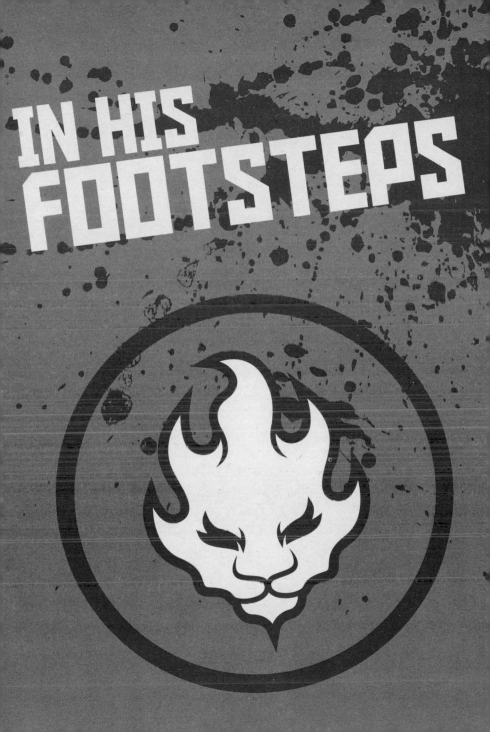

Kai crouched down, his brow knitted in concentration. His eyes were locked on the practice dummy ten feet away. It was just a thing of cloth and sticks, but it seemed to be making fun of him. He could almost hear it saying, "Ha! You call that a flying kick? You look like a chicken trying to fly . . . with one wing . . . blindfolded."

The young would-be ninja broke into a run. On his fifth stride, he planted his right foot and leaped into the air. His left foot was pointed straight out before him and aimed right at the target dummy's head. This time,

Kai would knock the head off. He was sure of it.

Just short of contact, he faltered. His left leg dropped perhaps half an inch, just enough to throw off his balance. He fought to correct it, but that only made the problem worse. Suddenly, his flying kick had turned into a confused jumble, arms and legs going every which way. Kai landed on his rear end, bounced, rolled, and wound up at the foot of the practice dummy.

Nearby, Sensei Wu looked on. After a moment, he began to slowly **clap his hands**. "Amazing," he said. "Not just anyone can botch a flying kick that badly. That takes real talent."

Kai got to his feet, brushing the dirt off his clothes. That had been his twelfth attempt at the maneuver, and his twelfth failure. He was angry at himself. His sister, Nya, was missing, captured by skeleton warriors, and she needed him to save her. And here he was

struggling to master the battle techniques he would need to know, while time was running out.

For the first time, he began to doubt. What if Sensei Wu had been wrong to choose him for training? What if he didn't have what it took to be a ninja, or to learn the art of Spinjitzu? Maybe he was just a blacksmith, as his father had been. Was he fooling himself that he could ever become a warrior?

"Try it again," repeated Sensei Wu, sipping from his cup of tea. Kai had never seen him actually make any tea, but he always seemed to have a cup of it on hand.

"What's the use?" Kai answered, his eyes on the ground. "Maybe I'm not cut out for this. Maybe I should go back to making swords and armor."

Sensei Wu smiled, remembering the incredibly bad sword he had seen Kai forge. "Yes, as I recall, you were a master at that."

Kai shot him a hard look. "Okay, so maybe

my work was a little . . . creative. At least I knew which end of the sword to put in the fire. Here? I'm not a ninja. I work in a blacksmith shop in a market square, just like my father did. I've lived in that village my whole life, the same as he did. We're just regular people. We're not **warriors and adventurers**."

Sensei Wu gently eased himself down onto a chair. He was looking in Kai's direction, but his eyes were focused on a past time. When he spoke, it was very quietly.

"Your father," Sensei Wu said, "did not live in that village all his life."

"What are you talking about?" asked Kai. "You told me that when you decided to hide the Four Weapons of Spinjitzu from your evil brother, you came to our village. You asked my father to draw a map showing the locations of the four hiding places."

"True," said Sensei Wu. "And from that day to this, I had never set foot in your village

again . . . because your father asked me not to."

Kai looked at the sensei in disbelief. "That's crazy. You're a sensei, a master of Spinjitzu, and you let a blacksmith tell you where you could and couldn't go?"

"No," Sensei Wu answered. "I respected the wishes of my best friend."

Seeing the expression on Kai's face, Sensei Wu smiled softly. "You look surprised. Did you not think Spinjitzu masters had friends? There was a time when your father and I traveled the length of this land, righting wrongs and aiding the weak. That was long before you were born, of course, or your sister."

"Are you saying my father knew **Spinjitzu**?"

Sensei Wu shook his head. "No. He could have, if he had chosen that path. But he did not."

There was an uncomfortable silence.

Finally, Kai sat down at Sensei Wu's feet and said, "I never knew any of this. Tell me about him . . . please."

"Your father was wise, brave, and the most trusted ally any man could have," Sensei Wu began. "We fought together for many years, sometimes even with Garmadon beside us, before my brother turned bad. We brought peace where there had been disorder. Your father was a hero, Kai."

The sensei smiled. "In the early days, he was much like you—headstrong, reckless. Once, we were searching for a group of samurai bandits. Your father was sure he saw them in a nearby field in the moonlight. Without waiting for me, he drew his sword and **charged**."

"What happened?" asked Kai.

"In the morning, we had to pay the farmer for all the scarecrows your father had 'defeated,'" the sensei said with a chuckle.

"As time passed, Garmadon and I grew

further apart. I came to rely on your father's advice and aid more and more. Yet another life beckoned to him. He had met and married the woman who would be your mother. Eventually, you and Nya were born. He chose to lay down his sword, settle in that village, and be with his family."

"Why?" asked Kai. "Why would he choose to live in a little out-of-the-way place when he had a life full of adventure?"

"I asked the same question, at the time," answered Sensei Wu. "Your father's answer was, 'Protecting the world begins with protecting the ones you love. There are many men who can wield a sword or win a battle. But only I can be a husband to my wife and a father to Kai and Nya.'"

Kai shrugged. It still didn't make sense to him. "And that was it? You two said good-bye?"

Sensei Wu nodded. "For a very long time, yes—where I traveled, danger traveled with me, and your father did not want his children put in jeopardy. When I finally defeated Garmadon and chose to hide the Weapons of Spinjitzu, I knew I had to share the secret of their location with someone I trusted."

"So you came to my father," said Kai.

"He made the map and hid it where we hoped no one would find it—inside the banner of your shop," Sensei Wu replied. "He knew it was a risk, keeping it there, but it was a greater one to allow it out of his sight. And I slept peacefully, knowing it was in his care."

"But Garmadon found it anyway."

Sensei Wu nodded. Kai said nothing for a long time. Finally, he looked up and asked, "Do you think my father would be proud of me?"

"If you try again, yes," Sensei Wu replied. "If you quit . . . that he would not understand. Your father chose to be a different kind of hero, a kind I could never be. He knew he was the only one who could raise you and

Nya and keep you strong and safe. And, Kai, you are the only one who can do what needs to be done now."

Kai stood and walked back to his start position. Once again, he concentrated on the training dummy. He pictured every movement he would make, from his leap to sailing straight and true through the air toward the target. But this time, as he began to run, he felt something more than a determination to succeed. He knew he was running in the footsteps of his father.

I will learn everything Sensei Wu can teach me, Kai thought as he took off into the air. *I will rescue Nya, Father. I will carry on your legacy and make you proud.*

There was no confusion, no wasted motion now — simply a young man with **fire in his heart** doing what he must do. He was one with his body, and the world around him seemed to slow down. Then his left foot landed on the target dummy,

punching through the straw and sticks and rags. The dummy toppled as Kai landed cleanly on his feet.

Sensei Wu gave the barest of smiles. "Better. Today, you fought your first great enemy—your own doubts—and you won. Take that victory into your tomorrows and you will bring honor to your name . . . and to the memory of your father."

"Whew!" said Kai. "After all that, I'm thirsty. Got any more of that tea?"

Sensei Wu smiled. "Snatch the cup from my hand without disturbing the tea inside . . . and we'll talk."

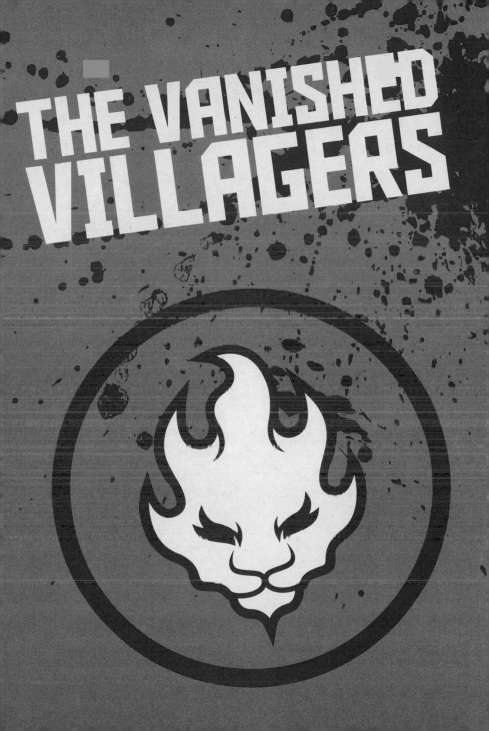

CHAPTER 1

Kai raised his axe and brought it down in one smooth motion, splitting a log with a loud crack. He had been chopping firewood for over an hour now and already had far more than was needed.

At least this makes me feel like I am doing something, thought the young ninja. *All this waiting around is going to drive me crazy!*

He put another log in place. As he lifted the axe, he imagined the log was the skeleton warrior who had kidnapped his sister, Nya. Kai had joined Sensei Wu's team in order to rescue her, but so far they had been mainly

23

concerned with finding the Four Weapons of Spinjitzu. Kai knew that was important—the Weapons had awesome power, after all—but it didn't feel like the search was getting him any closer to Nya. When he thought of her as a prisoner of Samukai and the skeleton legion, it made him want to explode with rage.

Kai swung the axe a little too hard this time and turned the log into splinters. He was just brushing them off his red garment when he heard a voice behind him.

"You should take it easy. What did that log ever do to you?"

It was Zane, the Ninja of Ice, leaning against a tree with his arms folded across his chest. His tone of voice, as always, was serious. The saying around camp was that Zane wouldn't know a joke if it bit him.

If someone else had made that remark, Kai might have snapped at him. But he had learned to accept that Zane was different,

even if he didn't always understand his fellow ninja. Zane honestly didn't seem to get why other people reacted to things the way they did, particularly when it came to anger or other strong emotions.

"I was thinking of . . . other things," Kai replied.

"Oh," said Zane. "And these other things are upsetting you?"

"What was your first clue?" said Kai, turning back to his work.

"It was the way you were chopping down a half dozen trees for one night's campfire," Zane answered calmly. "You should save your energy, Kai, for the fights to come."

Kai threw down the axe and sat down on a stump. "**What fights?** All we do is chase around Ninjago looking for . . . things. Meanwhile, my sister is out there somewhere in terrible trouble, waiting for me to save her, and what I am doing? Camping out!"

There was a long silence. Then Zane said softly, "I envy you."

Kai looked over his shoulder. He couldn't believe he had heard that correctly. "Envy me? What's to envy? My sister is missing because I wasn't fast enough or tough enough to save her from the skeletons."

Zane flashed the barest hint of a smile. "You don't understand. I don't envy the fact that your sister is missing — it's that you *know* she is missing. You have memories of her. That is more than I have."

Kai rose and walked over to his friend. He had heard fragments of the tale of Zane's past, but never in detail. *I've been so caught up in my own problems, I never stopped to think about what his might be,* Kai said to himself.

"Did you have a sister?" asked Kai.

"That's just it. I don't know," said Zane. "Not so very long ago, I woke up on a road outside of a small village. I had no memory of where I was or how I had gotten there. The people of the village took me in and gave me a home, but they couldn't tell me who I was. All I did remember was my name.

"I lived there until Sensei Wu came to me and offered me a place on this team. I thought that by **adventuring** I might uncover some clues to my past. So far, though, there hasn't been time to investigate."

Kai frowned. The sensei had often told him that worrying about his sister might distract him at some crucial moment. Yet he allowed Zane to go on missions when the ninja's entire past was a blank. Wouldn't that be at least a little distracting?

"How far away is that village?" asked Kai.

"Five or six miles, I would guess," answered Zane. "Why?"

"Because we are going to pay the place a visit," Kai replied. "Sensei Wu says we won't be moving on for a day or so anyway. That gives us time enough to check the place

out and see if we can find answers to some of your questions. Let's go."

As the two ninja headed back to camp to get their gear, neither noticed a shadow detach itself from the larger darkness. It belonged to a skeleton warrior, who was even now rushing back to the Underworld with most interesting news.

CHAPTER 2

amukai, leader of the skeleton legions, steepled his bony fingers and smiled. "Fascinating. It is a shame you missed the first part of the conversation, Kruncha, but what you did hear might prove useful."

Kruncha bowed his skull and tried hard to contain his excitement. Samukai was pleased! This might mean a promotion, or even permanent assignment to the world of Ninjago.

"If Kai and Zane are going to this village, then there must be something of importance there," Samukai continued. "They would not

take time from their mission for anything less than a critical quest. That means we must get there first."

Kruncha, eyes still on the ground, said, "But, wise and powerful Samukai, what if the two ninja arrive while we are searching for . . . whatever is there? The treasure might be destroyed in the battle . . . along with the two ninja, of course," he added hurriedly.

Samukai rose from his throne. "That is why we will distract the two would-be heroes, giving us all the time we need to find what they are seeking. Assemble a squad. Here is what we will do . . ."

Kai and Zane moved quickly through the woods. The ice on the tree limbs glittered like gems in the sunlight. The snow on the ground was topped with a thick coating of frost, which crunched loudly beneath Kai's feet. The fire ninja envied how Zane

could move over the snow so lightly that he **left no trace**.

"You'll have to teach me to do that," Kai said.

Zane shrugged. "I'm not sure I can."

"Didn't Sensei Wu teach it to you?"

"No," Zane answered. "I've always known how to do this. Or, at least, I woke up that day knowing how."

"And there wasn't anything on you that might have hinted at where you came from?" asked Kai. "No mud stains, pieces of plant, anything that could have shown where you were before?"

Zane shook his head. "I don't think so. But at the time, I was so confused that I really didn't pay much attention."

"You're not going to make this detective thing easy, I can see," Kai said, smiling.

Zane stopped and pointed up ahead. "Well, I think that's what you would call a clue."

Through the trees, Kai could see a small village. Smoke curled from a dozen chimneys and the air was filled with the sounds of men and women working and children playing. It reminded him of his own home. Somehow, that made him even more determined to help Zane.

The two ninja swiftly reached the outskirts of the village. Zane immediately saw someone he knew, a large, balding tinkerer named Genn.

"Hello!" said Zane. "It is good to see you again."

"Zane?" Genn said, glancing around, as if afraid someone might have heard him. Kai didn't know the man, but his behavior made the young ninja a little uneasy.

"What . . . um, what brings you here?" asked Genn.

"I just wanted to see my home again," said Zane. "This is my friend Kai."

Genn nodded in Kai's direction, but

his eyes never left Zane. There was fear in those eyes. "You picked a very bad time to come," the tinkerer said, a little too quickly. "You know how, ah, busy we are at this time of year. Maybe . . . maybe you would prefer visiting some other day."

"Is something the matter?" asked Zane.

Kai already knew what the man's answer would be, and that it would be a lie.

"No, of course not," said Genn. "Just . . . just a busy time, that's all."

"Then my friend and I can help and the work will go faster," Zane replied.

Kai and Zane walked into the village. Everywhere they went, they were met with looks of fear, anger, even despair. It didn't take a genius to see that something was very wrong. But whenever they asked, they were told everything was just fine.

Zane took Kai on a quick tour—the road on which he was found, the hut in which he had lived, and the icy lake he had been

meditating in on the day he met Sensei Wu. At first glance, Kai saw no clues to the mystery of Zane's past, but he had to admit he wasn't looking very hard. He was too distracted by the reactions of the villagers.

"Are they usually so disturbed around here?" asked Kai.

Zane leaned against a tree and folded his arms across his chest. "I have to admit, I have seen happier faces at funerals," he said.

"Yeah, well, let's make sure it's not our funeral that's being planned," said Kai. "From now on, **keep your eyes open**. Somebody's in real trouble here, and it might be us."

The two ninja spent the rest of the day chopping wood and doing other chores around the village. When they were done, they were ushered to the nicest hut in the village. Kai stood at the window of his room, watching the sunset, lost in thought. He wondered how Zane must feel being back here, where

everything was familiar and unfamiliar at the same time.

That night, the villagers held a feast for the heroes, or what passed for a feast in a place with little in the way of wealth or resources. Still, the people shared what little they had. Throughout the meal, no one seemed willing to look at either Kai or Zane in the eye. The conversation was strained and spoken in low tones. After a few hours, Kai began to feel very tired. He excused himself, went back to the hut, and fell sound asleep.

He awoke the next morning. The bright rays of dawn were streaming in his window. Kai stumbled out of bed, wondering why it was so quiet. Normally, in a village like this, people were up and working hard before sunrise. *Then again, this seems to be a pretty odd town,* he reminded himself.

Zane was just waking up. "I guess I am out of practice at doing anything but ninja training," he said. "About an hour after you left the dinner, I started to feel really tired. I came back here and fell right into bed."

"Must have been all that exciting

conversation at the party," Kai said. "And I guess it knocked everyone else out, too, because I don't hear anyone working."

Zane got out of bed, a look of concern on his face. "You're right, neither do I. But that makes no sense. Genn's right, this is the busiest time of the year for the village. Feast or no feast, they wouldn't sleep in."

He went out the door, Kai following. The two stood in the village square, looking around. There was no one around—nobody working, no children at play, not even a dog lying in the morning sun. Zane went straight to Genn's hut and knocked on the door. There was no answer.

Pushing the door open, Zane went inside. Breakfast was set on the table, tea and a hunk of bread. A fire was dying in the hearth. There was **no sign of anyone**. The two ninja searched the place and the surrounding area, but saw no sign of Genn or his family.

It was the same at every other house in the village. There was evidence of people having been in the homes just recently, but they were gone now. It seemed as if they had simply all disappeared at the same moment.

"I can't believe this," said Zane. "How could it have happened?"

"And why didn't it happen to us?" asked Kai.

"Maybe we should go get the sensei and Cole and Jay. What do you think?"

Kai shook his head. "I know how you feel, but it would take hours to get back to camp and then bring them back here. Sensei Wu might not even want to take time away from training for our mission to investigate. No, we need to solve this **OURSelves**."

Zane sat down on a bench, his head in his hands. "Kai . . . did we cause this?"

"What do you mean?"

"The people . . . they looked so afraid. Did someone or something target them because

we were here? Did we bring trouble to my home?"

Kai sat down next to him. "I don't know, Zane. But, whatever happened, we'll make it right. Whoever did this doesn't know what trouble is — but we're going to teach him."

CHAPTER

The first question the ninja had to try to answer, of course, was whether someone did something to the villagers or they did it to themselves. They had obviously been terrified of something, so the possibility existed that they had packed up and fled in the night.

"I could believe that, except for one thing," Zane said when Kai suggested the theory. "They didn't pack up. It doesn't look like anything's gone but the people."

"We're missing the easy answer," Kai replied. "Tracks — there's snow on the ground, so there have to be tracks showing where everyone went."

But there weren't any tracks. The two ninja searched the outskirts of the village, making a complete circle, and finding nothing beyond the marks left by squirrels and other small animals. In a number of places, there were faint lines in the snow, as if some kind of tool or machine had passed over. Whatever it had been, it hadn't been carrying people, as the lines weren't deep enough in the snow. Kai even tried climbing up on the roof of the tallest building, but all he could see in the distance was trees and snow. By the time he and Zane met up again, the Ninja of Fire was feeling extremely frustrated.

"**This is impossible!**" he snapped. "Even if they were taken, there would have to be some sign. They didn't just fly up into the sky and disappear."

"Maybe we're thinking about the wrong direction," Zane answered, pointing down to the ground. "Remember, Sensei Wu told us there are openings to the Underworld in various places. Maybe this is one of them. The skeletons could have stolen them away through such a portal, which would explain why there are no tracks leading out of the village."

Kai's expression turned grim. "So Samukai took them the same way he took my sister. Zane, we have to find that portal and get them back."

Zane nodded. "Agreed. What does a portal to the Underworld look like?"

Kai started to answer, then stopped. He suddenly realized he had no idea what such a thing would look like. It was pretty doubtful there would be a sign nearby reading, "This Way to the Underworld." As stupid as some of the skeletons were, even *they* weren't that dumb.

"Well, um, we'll know it when we see it, I'm sure," he answered finally.

The two began a methodical search of the village, checking every house and every patch of snow-covered ground for any sign of an entry point. All the while, Zane was troubled. It wasn't just the mystery of what had happened to his friends and neighbors. He knew worrying too much about them would distract him from spotting the answer to the puzzle. No, it was those lines he and Kai had seen in the snow all around the village. Their pattern seemed familiar somehow.

It was now late afternoon. Zane had run out of places to search. He went to find Kai to share the disappointing news that he had found nothing. He discovered his friend in a shed behind one of the huts, banging around among the owner's tools. Now and then, a hammer or a shovel would come **flying out** of the door.

"It has to be here," Kai was muttering. "They must have it well hidden. It's probably

under that pile of tools under there. No, I looked there already. . . ."

Cautiously, in case more tools came flying out, Zane opened the door to the shed. He was about to call out to Kai when he saw something hanging on the wall. Of course! It was so simple! No wonder they hadn't found any tracks.

"A rake!" he exclaimed.

"What? *Ow!*" said Kai, turning to see his friend and banging his head on a shovel in the process.

"The lines in the snow, the ones we saw all over," said Zane. "They were the marks left by a rake."

"Who rakes snow? Shovel it, sure, but rake it?" said Kai.

"Think about it," Zane continued. "If you had left footprints in the snow and wanted to obliterate them, what would you do? Run a rake over them. There were traces, all right, but someone went to a lot of trouble to hide them."

Kai smiled. "All right, now we have something. I'm not sure what, but it's something. Still, those marks were all over the outskirts. They don't tell us which direction the villagers went."

Zane hadn't thought of that. Still, it made sense. If they really wanted to keep things secret, it wouldn't make sense to only rake over one trail. That would stand out too much if it was spotted. It would be more effective to run the rakes all around the village so there would be no way to tell which concealed trail had been the right one.

"That's true," said the Ninja of Ice. "But perhaps—"

"**Quiet!**" Kai whispered. "I thought I heard something."

Now Zane heard it, too. Someone was sneaking around outside. They might have been making an effort to keep quiet, but the crunching snow was giving them away. He edged over toward the small window in

the rear of the shack. The glass was covered with a thick coating of frost, but Zane could just barely see that someone was moving around outside.

Zane signaled to Kai that he would try to distract the intruder while Kai slipped around the right side of the building to nab him. As soon as Kai snuck out the door, Zane said loudly, "No, Kai, I don't think we should just quit and go home. What? No, the people of this village don't play practical jokes. I really don't think—"

There were sounds of a scuffle coming from outside. Zane darted outside to see that Kai had transformed into a **fiery whirlwind** using the power of Spinjitzu, and was battering a skeleton warrior senseless with the snow and ice stirred up by his tornado. As Kai slowed down, Zane ran forward and grabbed the skeleton.

"What are you doing here?" Zane demanded. "Be warned, my friend here can do far worse than hurl snowballs at you."

The skeleton went from dazed to defiant in a matter of moments. "I won't tell you anything. I don't know anything."

"That I can believe," said Kai. "You guys aren't exactly hired for your brains . . . or your good looks, for that matter. Anyway, we don't need you to talk, we know what happened. You boneheads kidnapped the people of this village and now you want a ransom, right?"

The skeleton's face brightened. "Right . . . I mean, no. We didn't take the villagers. They, um, fled because they knew we were coming."

"And why were you coming to a tiny village like this?" pressed Zane. "What's here that Samukai could be interested in?"

The skeleton's jaws clamped shut. He had evidently remembered he wasn't supposed to be talking.

"Hey, Zane, do you know what's left of bone after a fire?" asked Kai.

"No, what?" answered Zane.

Kai leaned in very close to the skeleton warrior. "Not a whole lot."

"Okay, okay!" said the skeleton. "It's . . . it's . . ." He dropped his voice to a whisper. "It's the treasure."

Kai and Zane looked at each other, then back at their prisoner, confused. "What treasure?" asked Zane.

"There's a legion on its way to get it," the skeleton hissed. "We know just where it is in the village."

"Then why don't you tell us, and we'll all know," said Kai. "Zane, do you know anything about a treasure hidden here?"

Zane shook his head. "No, but I would certainly like to hear more."

The skeleton warrior suddenly wrenched himself loose from the grasp of the ninja and started running toward the shed. Before Kai or Zane could stop him, he dove through the small window and into the building.

"Well, that was a silly thing to do," said Kai as the two ninja ran around to the front of the shed. "Does he think we won't be able to find him?"

Zane grabbed Kai and shoved him down to the ground. "I think he was counting on us finding him. Duck!"

A thrown axe **sliced the air** just above the ninja's heads. It was followed by shovels, rakes, and knives, all hurled through the open door of the shed by the skeleton warrior inside. The storm of tools kept the two ninja pinned down.

"He has to run out of ammunition eventually," said Kai.

"What if his aim gets better in the meantime?" Zane answered. "I have an idea."

The Ninja of Ice sprang to his feet, braced for battle. As the sharp tools flew at him, he batted them aside with eye-blurring speed. Then, somehow, he missed a strike. A hammer made it past his defenses and struck him a glancing blow on the head. Zane hit the ground hard and lay still.

"Zane! Are you all right?" said Kai.

The Ninja of Ice opened one eye. **"Shhhh.** It just looked like the hammer hit me, but don't let our friend inside know that. Now you try."

Kai jumped up and ran for the shed. He made it halfway there before a thrown shovel brought him down, or seemed to. Like Zane, he lay still and quiet in the snow.

After a few minutes, the skeleton warrior peeked out the door of the shed. Seeing both his enemies were unconscious, he smiled. Samukai would certainly reward him for finishing off two such dangerous foes. He picked up a shovel and took a step toward where Kai was sprawled on the ground.

Then he stopped and thought. *Didn't Samukai say something about these ninja?* **What was it?** *Leave them a lamp? Leave them a loaf? No, no, that wasn't*

*it. I know it was important. Leave them . . .
leave them . . .*

Alive! That's it. Leave them alive!

He dropped the shovel. It landed on his foot, making him yell so loud he almost startled Kai into moving. Grumbling, the skeleton hobbled off to the east and was soon out of the village.

As soon as he was gone, Zane and Kai got to their feet. Keeping behind the cover of buildings, they watched as the skeleton limped toward the woods.

"Once he is inside the forest, we will trail him," said Zane. "I still think the skeletons captured my friends for some reason and he will lead us right to them."

"So you don't think there's a treasure here?" asked Kai.

Zane gestured toward the simple huts all around. "Does it *look* like there's a treasure here?"

"Hey, my blacksmith shop just looked like

51

a blacksmith shop," Kai replied. "How was I to know a map to the Four Weapons of Spinjitzu was hidden there? You never know what someone might think is a good hiding place."

Zane wasn't paying attention. His eyes were on the skeleton warrior, who was now about fifty yards from the edge of the woods. Then, to the ninja's amazement, the skeleton simply disappeared.

The two ninja raced to the spot where the warrior had last been seen. The skeleton's footprints in the snow abruptly stopped, but there was nowhere nearby he could be hiding. He was just gone.

"Come on, we'll search the woods," Kai said. "He must be here somewhere."

"The sun's setting," Zane answered. "It will be pitch-dark in a few minutes. We won't spot him and we might be walking into an ambush. Better to wait for morning."

"The sun's setting," Kai repeated. "The sun's . . . **Wait a minute!** Something isn't right here!"

Kai ran back into the village, straight to the house he and Zane were sharing. He ran to his window and stared out at the darkness. "I can't see it. That explains everything."

"Can't see what? I don't know what you're talking about," said Zane.

"The sunset," said Kai. "Last night, I saw the sun setting outside this window. But this morning, I saw the sun *rising* outside this same window."

"That's impossible," said Zane. "That would mean the window was facing west at night—"

"—and east in the morning," Kai finished for him. "A lot of 'impossible' things have been happening around here, and I think now I know why."

Zane frowned. "So it's not the same window?"

"You're thinking too small," said Kai,

smiling. "It's not the same house. It's not the same village. We've been tricked, Zane. The only thing I'm not sure of is why."

The two ninja stayed up all night, keeping watch for an attack by the skeletons. None came. In the morning, Kai led Zane back to the spot where they had seen the skeleton disappear.

"They couldn't afford to move us too far from where we had been before, or we might have noticed that the stars were all different," the Ninja of Fire explained. "But they had to make sure we couldn't see the answer. **Stand back.**"

Kai picked up a rock and threw it with all his might toward the woods. Fifty yards short of the line of trees, it struck something and dropped to the ground. Zane's eyes widened as a spiderweb of cracks suddenly appeared in empty space. He went to the spot where the rock had impacted and reached out. Where he would have expected to feel nothing but cold air, he instead felt a smooth, hard surface.

"It's a mirror," said Kai, "a big one, too. There are probably others around as well. Makes it look like there's just trees and snow all over. Our pal didn't vanish—he just slipped behind the mirror."

"Then that is where we're going, too," said Zane.

CHAPTER 5

Samukai smacked the skeleton warrior who stood before him with two of his four hands. Then he smacked him with the other two for good measure.

"Idiot," the ruler of the Underworld growled. "Dumb pile of bones. I gave you a simple job, and you screwed it up."

"But, Master, I defeated them in battle and successfully escaped," the skeleton whined. "I thought you would be pleased."

Samukai sat down hard on his throne of bones. "Understand something: The day I want Kai and Zane defeated, it will

happen without aid from you. The point of this exercise was not a test of strengths, but a masterpiece of deception."

It had, truly, been one of Samukai's most inspired ideas. He knew two of Sensei Wu's ninja would not be visiting a tiny village just for fun. There had to be some treasure concealed there that Wu wanted to get his hands on. He could have simply had skeletons keep an eye on Kai and Zane and pounce when they grabbed the treasure, but what if one of the villagers took it and hid it in the meantime? No, he had to know the precise location of the ninja's goal and then be able to get it without their interference.

And so he put his plan into action. First, Kruncha and a large group of skeleton warriors **descended** on the village. While a few remained behind to make sure the villagers behaved, the rest went to work building a duplicate of the village not far away. Giant mirrors would keep the ninja from spotting any signs of the real village when they were in the fake one.

Unfortunately, Kruncha's bumblers were not yet done when Kai and Zane arrived. At Kruncha's direction, the villagers made the ninja welcome, or as welcome as frightened humans could. That night, during the feast, they gave the two ninja tea with certain herbs in it that put them to sleep. The skeletons then transported Kai and Zane to the fake village.

The plan was simple. The ninja would wake up and be faced with the mystery of the disappearing villagers. Fearful, they would race to retrieve the treasure, not knowing they were being spied upon by the skeletons. Once the hiding place was revealed, Samukai would be notified and his warriors would get the treasure from its place of concealment in the real village.

The ninja surprised the skeletons. They did not go searching for the treasure, but the villagers. Impatient, Samukai sent a warrior in

with instructions to get captured and further motivate the ninja to get the treasure. That had not worked out well.

"They will be on their way there," muttered Samukai, "in search of the treasure. And as soon as they have it . . . we will take it away from them."

CHAPTER 6

When Kai and Zane slipped around behind the giant mirror, they should not have been surprised by the sight that greeted their eyes . . . yet, still, they were. There, not far in the distance, was Zane's village. It had been so close all the time and they had never been aware of it.

"Let's go," said a determined Zane. "Someone is going to pay for tricking us."

"Not so fast," said Kai. "Look."

On the outskirts of the village, skeleton warriors were patrolling in pairs. Beyond them, villagers could be seen working under the watchful eye sockets of more skeletons. The little town was now an armed camp.

"I see," said Zane. "If we go charging in there, innocents might get hurt. But we can't just leave them all to be prisoners of the skeletons."

"What does Sensei Wu always tell us? 'Use your opponent's strength against him,'" answered Kai. "Well, what do the skeletons want? Based on what our ex-captive said, they think there's treasure in the village. They probably also think we know where it is. So let's **lead them to it**."

Zane looked at his friend, puzzled. "How? There is no treasure."

Kai smiled. "But they don't know that. Come on, we have a lot of work to do."

By that evening, the two ninja were ready. Carrying shovels, they slipped into the woods close to the edge of the real village. They crouched down by a pair of tree stumps

and watched the skeletal guards on patrol for a few moments. Then Kai whispered, "Stay here."

The Ninja of Fire got to his feet and moved off, purposely letting the moonlight reveal him to the skeletons. The two warriors immediately started following Kai into the woods.

My friend was right, thought Zane. *They didn't attack him. They want to know where he's going and what he might find there.*

Once Kai was sure he was being followed, he started walking faster. Then he began to run. Behind him, the skeletons were running, too. They knew that losing sight of the ninja now would mean punishment from Samukai.

Kai spotted the old, rotted log he and Zane had left as a marker. He picked up speed and **leaped**, landing in the snow about ten feet past the log. He turned to see the pair of skeletons jumping over the log. There was a series of sharp cracks and the two warriors disappeared from view, falling into the concealed pit Kai and Zane had dug. Some sticks and some snow had hidden it well until it was too late.

"That's two down," said Kai.

🔥 🔥 🔥

Not far away, Zane had his own trap set. Once he was certain he had attracted skeleton attention, he went to work. Scurrying halfway up a hillside, he came to a natural rock wall. He immediately started banging one of the large rocks with his shovel, attempting to wrestle it free, and muttering angrily about how stubborn the stupid piece of stone was turning out to be. Finally, he threw up his hands in seeming frustration and stalked off.

Once he was well clear of the spot, Zane hid to watch what would happen. After a few minutes, a pair of skeletons raced over to the wall and wrenched the rock free. They had about two seconds to feel proud of their accomplishment before the entire wall

collapsed on them, followed by the ton of snow the wall had been holding back.

Satisfied they would be digging themselves out for the rest of the night, Zane moved on to his next targets.

🔥 🔥 🔥

For the next three hours, Kai and Zane whittled down the numbers of the skeleton warriors. Now it was getting tricky. Samukai, Kruncha, and three skeletons were in the town meeting hall, along with all the villagers. Two other skeletons were in the center of town, mounted on a Turbo Shredder vehicle. The fearsome machine, with its skull grill and chomping, front-mounted "jaws," could end the ninja's night in a big hurry.

"I know how to get the villagers free," said Zane. "But we need the Shredder to do it. Any ideas?"

Kai smiled. "Let's head for the toolshed. I think it's time to chop some wood."

Later, Zane sat high in a tree, ready to

spring their trap. Down on the ground, Kai was calculating distance. "Okay, when I pass Genn's house, you need to start cutting," the Ninja of Fire said. "The timing has to be just right, or else Sensei Wu is going to be short two ninja."

"Good luck," said Zane.

Kai waved and ran off into the village. He raced right up to the Turbo Shredder and started jumping up and down, saying, "You guys couldn't catch a cold! The other ninja wanted to help, but I told them I could handle twenty skeletons by myself. What did you think, that you snuck into this village without us noticing? We could hear your **bones rattling** a hundred miles away!"

The skeleton driver gunned the Turbo Shredder to life. Kai wheeled and ran for the woods, the vehicle on his heels. He could hear the jaws clamping down behind him and knew that if he so much as stumbled, he

wouldn't be getting up again. He sped past Genn's house, hoping that Zane saw him and was sawing away.

The Ninja of Ice had indeed spotted his friend. Counting down to himself, he sliced the thick ropes he and Kai had rigged up. He had just finished when Kai ran past, followed closely by the Turbo Shredder. The last strand of rope gave way then and the huge tree trunk the two ninja had rigged swung free.

The skeletons never knew what hit them. The tree trunk slammed into the Turbo Shredder, sending it rolling onto its side and hurling the two warriors out into the snow. Kai knocked them out with two well-placed chops as Zane scrambled down the tree.

"Help me get this thing back on its treads," said Kai. "Then we'll go pay a call on Samukai."

CHAPTER 7

Kai stood in front of the town hall. Light blazed within the building and he could hear the soft cries of children coming from inside. He wanted to march right in and pound Samukai and his skeletons for scaring all these innocent people, but better to stick to the plan. The important thing was getting Genn and the others out safe.

"Hey, skullface!" he shouted at the closed doors. "I have something you want!"

The door opened a crack. Kruncha poked his skull out. "Uh, like what?"

Kai shook his head. "I only talk to your

boss. Let's see his ugly face." When Kruncha hesitated, Kai added, "Or I could just take the treasure back to Sensei Wu like I'm supposed to."

Kruncha withdrew. An instant later, the door opened wider. Samukai, all four arms and fierce expression, appeared. He took a moment to size Kai up, and then said, "Where is it? And what is it?"

"Where you won't find it," answered Kai. "And you'll find out what it is when you get it, which you will . . . in exchange for the villagers."

"Sensei Wu is getting soft in his old age." Samukai chuckled. "Trading a treasure for a few dozen humans? And not even human warriors?"

"Some of us think all humans are important," Kai replied. "We're funny that way. Do we have a deal?"

"First, show me the treasure."

"No," said Kai. "First, show me the villagers.

I want to be sure you haven't . . . lost any."

"Fair enough." Samukai nodded. He barked an order to someone behind him. Then he flung the doors open wide. The villagers were all crowded in behind him, just where Kai wanted them.

"Now!" shouted the Ninja of Fire.

There was a roar like an angry dragon and then Zane smashed the Turbo Shredder through the back wall of the town hall. Skeleton warriors were scattered like leaves in a windstorm. The villagers surged forward, pushing Samukai ahead of them.

"Go! Run!" yelled Kai. "Get as far from here as you can!"

Inside the building, Zane was turning the Turbo Shredder this way and that, chewing up floor and furniture as the skeletons fled in terror. Two jumped out the windows while the third scrambled into the chimney and tried to climb up toward the roof (only to get stuck halfway).

Samukai got to his feet and brushed the snow off himself with his four hands. He glanced at the chaos inside the town hall, then at the fleeing villagers, and finally at Kai. "No treasure?"

"Guess not," said Kai.

"Then why did you and your friend come here?"

"I don't think you would understand," said Kai. "It's a human thing."

Samukai shrugged. "Probably not. You realize I could destroy you and your friend?"

Kai slipped into **battle-ready stance**. "I realize you could try."

The ruler of the Underworld smiled. It was a ghastly sight. "But if there is no treasure, there would be no point. We will meet each other again, little ninja, and all questions will be answered. For now, I see no need to soil my hands in combat with you. Oh, and you might tell your friend to turn off the engine. I am sure these people would like a town hall

to return to, for the little time that is left to them."

Before Kai could respond, Samukai had vanished. *Evidently, I was right about one thing,* the ninja thought. *There is a portal to the Underworld in this town.*

CHAPTER

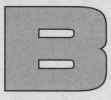y the next morning, the villagers had returned. Most looked ashamed for the part they had played in tricking the ninja.

"We had no choice," said Genn. "But that doesn't make it any better."

"It turned out all right," Zane assured him. "Kai and I have to move on, but I will be back to check on all of you. I don't think the skeletons will come back again. If they do, Kai and I will give them a proper welcome."

Genn gave Zane a hug. The other villagers came up to shake the ninja's hands, pat them on the back, and thank them for their

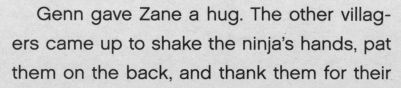

help. When everyone had had their say, Kai and Zane turned and left the village.

"Imagine those stupid skeletons," Kai said, laughing, "thinking there was some great treasure hidden there."

"Well, there was," Zane replied. "But they never would have recognized it."

"What do you mean?"

Zane looked back at the village. "Each and every one of those villagers welcomed me — a stranger — into their community. They gave me shelter and food and friendship. When I left, I did so knowing that if I ever needed to come back, they would take me in. That makes them the closest thing I have to family in this world."

Kai thought about his sister. She was all the family he had left in the world, and there was nothing he would not do for her. **"I get it,"** he said, "and you're right, Zane — that is a treasure."

The two walked on in silence for a while

before Kai said, "Hey. We got so wrapped up in solving the mystery in the village that we never learned anything about your past."

"I know," said Zane. "I still want to . . . need to . . . learn where I came from. But maybe for today, it is enough to think about where I am and with whom. Whoever I was before, it led me to good friends and a life with purpose. For the moment, I don't need more than that."

"Then let's get back," said Kai. "Maybe if we tell our tale well enough, Sensei Wu will forget to punish us for being gone so long."

"You don't really believe that," said Zane.

Kai did his best to look very serious. Then his expression cracked and he burst out laughing. "No, no, I really don't. We are so in for it, but **at least we got a good story out of all this**."

ZANE: NINJA OF ICE

By Greg Farshtey

SCHOLASTIC INC.

New York   Toronto   London   Auckland
Sydney   Mexico City   New Delhi   Hong Kong

ISBN 978-0-545-39822-0

12 11 10 9 8 7 6 5 4 3 2 1   11 12 13 14 15 16/0

Printed in the U.S.A.   40
First printing, August 2011

CONTENTS

FROM THE JOURNAL OF SENSEI WU........ 1

GETTING THE JOKE..................... 9

THE CHOICE.......................... 23

    CHAPTER 1...................... 25

    CHAPTER 2...................... 29

    CHAPTER 3...................... 33

    CHAPTER 4...................... 37

    CHAPTER 5...................... 43

    CHAPTER 6...................... 50

    CHAPTER 7...................... 54

    CHAPTER 8...................... 60

    CHAPTER 9...................... 67

    CHAPTER 10 74

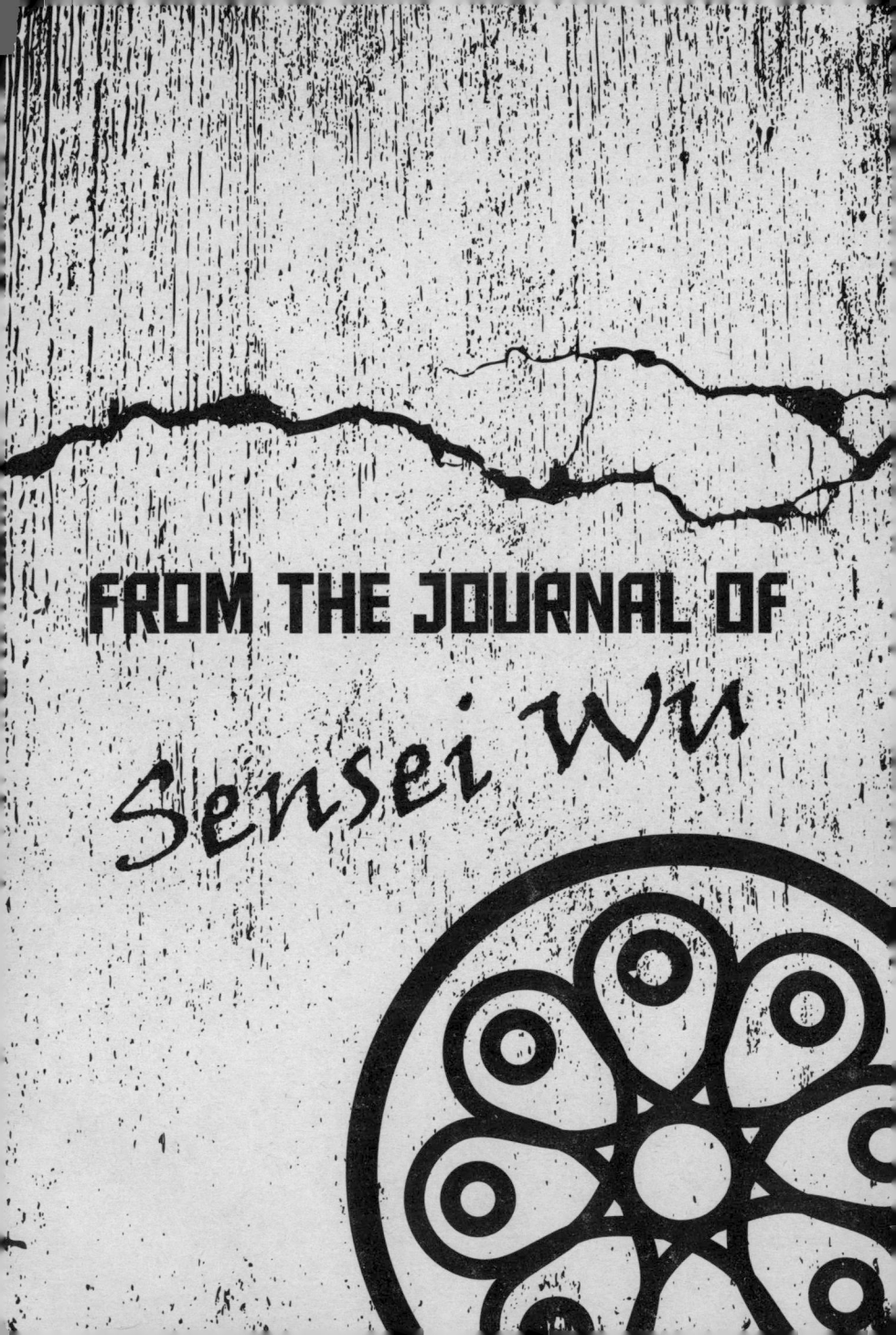

FROM THE JOURNAL OF

Sensei Wu

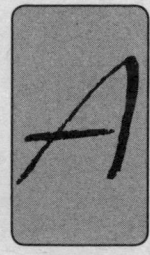*A*h, Zane . . . will I ever solve the mystery that surrounds him? More important, will he ever learn the answers to all his questions? Sometimes, I fear not.

I had first heard rumors some time ago about a youth in a northern province capable of withstanding extreme cold. At the time, my other duties kept me from seeking him out. When my brother, Garmadon, threatened to steal the Four Weapons of Spinjitzu, I was forced to seek out potential ninja. This caused my path to finally cross that of Zane.

I found him in a most unusual place. He was sitting at the bottom of an icy lake, meditating. On the shore, a crowd of villagers had gathered, all of them marveling at how long Zane had managed to stay underwater. Anyone else would surely have surfaced after a few minutes due to lack of air or the freezing cold, but Zane seemed to be hardly bothered by either condition. He was, however, quite shocked to open his eyes and see me seated down there with him.

Zane was an orphan . . . or, rather, he thought he might be but was not sure. As it turned out, he was a young man without a past. He said he had awakened one day near his village with no memory of how he had gotten there or where he had been before. All he knew was his name. He made his way into the village and earned a living doing jobs for various people. The fact that Zane was able to do work outdoors in brutally cold conditions

made him much valued, especially by those who preferred to stay indoors by the fire during snowstorms.

When I asked him about training to be a ninja, he was slow to say yes at first. As we talked, he realized that there were many secrets he could uncover through this training. That was how I discovered that Zane loves to learn and is always trying to find out new things.

Zane is, in fact, possibly the smartest of my four ninja. That is, if you measure how smart someone is only by what they have learned from books. Zane can tell you why the grass is green, how a flower grows, what makes a babbling brook sound the way it does. But I have never known him to lie in the grass and look at the clouds, smell a flower, or relax by a brook. I have seen him study the structure of a snowflake, but I wonder if he sees the beauty in the fact that no two are alike?

My other ninja — Jay, Cole, and Kai —
have certainly noticed that Zane is a bit
different from them. They talk about how he
has no sense of humor. He rarely smiles and
never laughs and doesn't seem to even get
the jokes the other young men tell. Although
they like him and respect him, it is
sometimes hard for them to feel close to
Zane. There is something about him that just
feels . . . unique, and no one can identify
what it is.

Despite his dedication to his training and
the mission, I know Zane is troubled by the
questions about his past. He wants to know
the answers, but perhaps he fears them as
well. What if his parents are still alive and
searching for him? Or what if they are
bandits and would want him to use his skills
for crime? What if the story of his early years
holds the key to everything about him that
seems so strange to others?

Still, he has shown me again and again
that he was the right choice to be my Ninja of
Ice. When he faces an enemy, he seeks out
points of weakness and targets them. When
he strikes, it is not out of anger or fear. Even
when faced with a mighty Ice Dragon, Zane
does not panic. I have seen Kai let his love
for his sister blind him to danger, and Jay's
humor desert him in a moment of crisis. But
Zane is ice.

What does the future hold for this most
mysterious of ninja? I do not know. I believe
he hopes his adventures with Kai and the
others will somehow lead him to answers
about his past. I truly believe he would go to
the ends of the world to find out who he really is — and I and my ninja will stand beside
him as he searches for clues to this greatest
of mysteries.

GETTING THE JOKE

Zane picked his way carefully down the rocky hillside. His eyes had already adjusted to the darkness, but it would still have been easy to trip and fall. If he were to tumble and cry out, he might be warning Samukai's skeleton warriors that the ninja were nearby. Worse, if he was badly injured, Sensei Wu and Zane's three friends would have to leave him behind. The mission they were on was too dangerous and too important to risk its success.

The "mission" Zane was undertaking at the moment seemed far less important.

Sensei Wu had sent him off to gather sticks so a fire could be built. Although it was a cold evening in the mountains, Zane didn't see the sense in making a campfire. They were very close to the Caves of Despair, the place Sensei was sure would be teeming with skeleton warriors. Why build a fire and potentially give away their position? Not for the first time, Zane wondered if the sensei truly knew what he was doing.

The hillside suddenly grew much steeper. Zane found himself running faster than he wanted to toward the bottom, and only reaching out for a nearby tree slowed him. He glanced up and noted there were a number of branches that would make good firewood. As silently as possible, he began to climb the tree.

There could, of course, have been another good reason why the sensei sent him off on this task. He had been traveling with the other ninja — Cole, Jay, and Kai — for days

now, but he did not really fit in with them. Despite the danger they all were facing, the three youths were always **laughing and joking**. Zane never joined in. In fact, he couldn't remember ever really doing that. He had always been a serious person, devoted to meditation, and hadn't had time for humor and games.

The others didn't know that about him. All they saw was someone who didn't "get" the joke. Maybe they were beginning to wonder if Zane was afraid of the challenges ahead of them, and that was why he was so grim. If they had doubts about him, it might cause problems in battle. Maybe the sensei wanted time alone with the three to discuss this, so he sent Zane off on a pointless job.

Zane didn't think he was afraid. He certainly respected the power of Garmadon and Samukai; only a fool would not. But the feelings that came with fear—cold sweat, trembling, heart pounding—were absent

from him. Much of what the ninja would face was still unknown, and Zane saw no point in fearing the unknown. It was a waste of energy.

He was about to break off a small branch when he heard a twig **snap** down below. Flattening himself against the tree trunk, he waited and watched. In a few moments, he saw the moonlight gleaming off the polished bones of a skeleton warrior. The skeleton was alone and muttering to himself as he walked.

"'Go get the wood, Nuckal,'" grumbled the skeleton. "'Pick up those rocks, Nuckal.' 'Stop eating all the donuts, Nuckal.' Orders, orders, orders, that's all I ever hear."

Zane knew what he had to do. This Nuckal might stumble upon the camp and see Sensei Wu and the others. He would then rush back and report to Samukai. If the skeletons found out about the ninja now, it would be a disaster. The success of the mission depended on surprise.

He waited until Nuckal was right under the tree. Then Zane let go of the trunk and jumped down on top of the skeleton. Nuckal let out an **"OOF"** as Zane landed on him, and the two rolled around on the ground until they smacked into a big rock. Zane was stunned for an instant, allowing the skeleton to get to his bony feet.

"Ha!" said Nuckal. "You're my prisoner!"

Zane rolled aside and sprang into a crouch, a shuriken in his hand. "No. You are my prisoner."

"I said it first," insisted Nuckal.

"I hardly think that matters," Zane answered. "I have a shuriken. You dropped your sword fifteen-point-two feet up the hill. How can I be your prisoner if you have no weapon?"

Nuckal smiled and tapped his head with a long finger of bone. "I have my brain . . . well, actually, I don't really, but I'll bet I'm still smarter than you."

"Why would you think that?" asked Zane.

"For one thing, when I climb trees, I don't fall out of them," Nuckal said, with pride in his voice. "And I don't **run around in the dark** by myself in the middle of the night where I might run into trouble."

"Actually, I am pretty sure that is what you were doing when we met," Zane replied.

"Shows what you know," snapped Nuckal. "When you work for Samukai, you're never alone. Someone is always watching you to make sure you don't eat all the donuts."

Zane frowned. "How can you eat donuts when you have no stomach?"

Nuckal started to answer, then paused, looking confused. A moment later, he opened his mouth again to speak, and stopped again, seeming even more puzzled than before. He looked down at the ground and scratched his skull. Finally, he glared at Zane and said, "That's none of your business!"

"Turn around," said Zane. "I am taking you back to my friends."

Nuckal shook his head. "*You* turn around. Samukai will want to talk to you."

Zane threw his shuriken. It glanced off Nuckal's skull and into the woods. The skeleton **staggered** for a second, but his bone was like armor so he wasn't harmed. Then the two began to fight furiously. First one was winning, then the other, but they were too evenly matched for either to win. They were rolling around on the grass when Nuckal hit his head on a rock and stopped fighting, dazed.

Zane got to his feet. *If I knew Spinjitzu, I could win, but I don't yet. We could fight all night, and if I lost, it would put the others in danger. Still, he's not too bright, so maybe . . .*

"You can't capture me," Zane said suddenly. **"I'm not really here."**

"Huh?" said Nuckal. "But you fell out of a tree and now you're standing right there."

"A tree?" Zane said in disbelief. "Did you ever hear of a ninja falling out of a tree before?"

"Well . . . no," Nuckal admitted.

"Then it doesn't make sense that one did tonight," said Zane. "Want to know what really happened?"

Nuckal nodded. Zane couldn't tell if the skeleton was genuinely starting to disbelieve his own eyes or just waiting to see how far the ninja would push this, but he pressed on anyway.

"You were in your camp," said Zane. "Someone told you to go out and look for wood."

"Sure, Kruncha did," said Nuckal.

"Just before you left, Kruncha told you a joke," said Zane. "Ummmm . . . how did the ninja get up in the tree?"

Nuckal brightened. "I don't know, how?"

"He hid inside an acorn and let a squirrel carry him up," said Zane, doing his best to sound the way Jay did when he told a joke.

Nuckal laughed. **"Ha!** An acorn! Some big ninja hiding inside a little acorn . . . that's a good one."

Zane took a step backward. "Right. In fact, you were thinking about that joke the whole time you were walking here."

"I was?"

Zane took another step back. "Sure. Think about it—a little squirrel carrying a ninja up a tree. That's funny."

The ninja wasn't really sure if it was funny or not, but he had heard Cole tell the joke once and the others had laughed. Nuckal certainly seemed to like it, as he started laughing even harder this time.

"So there you were, minding your own business, thinking about the joke, when you tripped and hit your, um, skull on a rock," Zane continued. "Naturally, you got all

confused. When you got up, you thought you really were seeing a ninja who had been up in a tree. But, of course, you weren't."

"Right," said Nuckal. "Of course. That would be ridiculous. **A ninja up a tree?** You would have to be really stupid to believe that."

Zane took another step back. He was almost completely hidden by darkness now. "One more thing: I wouldn't tell anyone back at your camp about what you thought you saw. They wouldn't understand."

"Yeah, they wouldn't . . . ," Nuckal began. But the ninja he had been talking to—well, the one he imagined he had been talking to—was gone.

Shrugging, the skeleton turned around and started picking up sticks to bring back to camp. It had certainly been a strange night, but he was glad that the imaginary ninja had been nice enough to admit he wasn't real. It would have been embarrassing to tell

Kruncha he had seen someone who clearly wasn't there.

❊ ❊ ❊

Zane had gathered an armful of wood and was on his way back to camp. No doubt the others would be waiting for him. He looked forward to telling them about his adventure . . . and that, maybe, he finally got the joke.

CHAPTER 1

Zane sat at the bottom of a half-frozen pond, eyes closed, meditating. The water was so bitterly cold that the average person would have been shocked into unconsciousness by exposure to it, but Zane was not bothered at all. He had taught himself how to put the sensation of cold out of his mind, just as he mastered how to slow his breathing. This allowed him to stay underwater for an extraordinary length of time.

The last chance he'd had to meditate this way had been in his village. He had been at the bottom of an icy lake then, when he

opened his eyes to see the amazing sight of Sensei Wu, teacup in hand, down there with him. That was when the sensei recruited him to join his team of ninja. Their mission was to stop the evil Lord Garmadon from getting his hands on the Four Weapons of Spinjitzu. So far, they had retrieved two of the four artifacts.

Now, as he pondered in the frigid water, Zane wondered if he had made the right choice in joining Wu's team. True, what they were doing was vitally important to the safety of the world of Ninjago. But Zane had joined for other reasons besides fighting for justice. He had hoped that the chance to travel the world would lead him to answers about his past.

Thus far, that effort had produced no results, and the fact gnawed at him. The frustration he felt at the thought of his failure actually broke his concentration. Suddenly, his lungs were **burning**. He had to

rush to the surface and get a breath of air. Clawing his way back onto shore, he inhaled deeply.

Zane looked around. He was alone. But that was not unusual. In a sense, he was alone wherever he went — for without memories, what does a man have? Zane had awakened one day on a road outside a small village, with no idea how he had gotten there or where he was. He knew his name and little else. The people of the village had taken him in and there he had stayed until Sensei Wu's arrival. Since then, he had been haunted by questions: Who was he? Where had he come from? The answers remained elusive.

Not long ago, he and his friend Kai had traveled back to that village in search of clues to Zane's past. Instead of finding any answers, they found themselves in the middle of a plot by Samukai, ruler of the Underworld, and his skeleton warriors. The two ninja had

smashed the plan, but found nothing to fill in the gaps in Zane's memories.

Zane stood up. There was no point in regrets, he decided. A commitment had been made to Sensei Wu and he had to live up to it. Perhaps when Ninjago was safe from Garmadon, there would be time to resume his search for his past.

Zane was about to leave the pond and head back to camp when he heard a noise nearby. It sounded like a low moan, as if someone were in pain. Zane stopped and listened intently. Yes, it was coming from a cave nearby. The ninja sprinted off in the direction of the sound.

The cave mouth was small and narrow. Zane noted that if the cave itself was the same size, there would be little room to maneuver in a fight. In a split second, he ran down a list of what might be causing the noise. Someone might have been hurt by an animal inside the cave; someone might have been exploring the cave and been injured; the noise might be coming from a wounded animal of some sort; the sound might even be caused by the wind blowing through a gap in the rock somewhere.

Naturally, there was one other possibility:

It was a trap. Samukai had already tried tricking Zane and Kai to get what he thought was a treasure. He might try it again.

Zane stood at the edge of the cave entrance and called out, "**Is someone in there?** Are you hurt?"

Silence was the only answer.

A voice came from the darkness of the cave. "Help me. . ." It was a man's voice, faint, as if the person it belonged to was very weak or badly hurt.

Zane didn't hesitate. There was no time to go for help. If someone was injured, he had to aid them, even if it meant risking an ambush. Now with the power of Spinjitzu at his command, he figured the odds were on his side even if it was a trap.

He took a few cautious steps inside, allowing his eyes to adjust to the darkness. The sounds had stopped. Zane peered into the cave, hoping to spot whoever had been calling for help. He saw no one.

"You won't find me here," the voice said, stronger now. "But I do require your help."

Zane looked around, his hands already curling into fists. "Where are you? **Show yourself.**"

"The answer to the first is the reason I cannot do the second," the voice replied. "I cannot come to you, Zane. You must come to me."

"Thanks," said Zane, turning around. "I'll pass. Somehow, I have the feeling the cost of helping you would be a little too high."

The ninja intended to head for the exit, but there was nothing there but darkness now. He couldn't see a way out. Still, he did not panic. That wasn't Zane's way. If this was an elaborate trap—and maybe even his last battle—he would still face it calmly. As Sensei Wu always said, an angry fighter has already lost the war.

"I am afraid I cannot let you leave until you have heard me out," the voice said gently.

"All I ask is that you listen. No harm will come to you, Zane. If I wanted you dead . . . well, you would be begging for death by now."

Zane turned back toward the direction from which the voice was coming. "Since I don't seem to be going anywhere, say what you have to say. Start with who you are."

A soft chuckle filled the cave. "Don't you know?"

Then the laughter was drowned out by the sound of rock scraping against rock. A crack of light appeared on the cavern floor in front of Zane, growing wider and wider as he watched. When the noise finally stopped, a portion of the stone floor had slid away to reveal a winding staircase.

"I am the stuff of your **night-mares**," said the voice. "I am the bogeyman in all of Sensei Wu's bedtime stories. I am the exile, the outcast, the villain that every tale must have . . . I am Garmadon."

CHAPTER 3

As Zane climbed down the stairs, he did his best to convince himself it was a wise thing to do. If he could confront Garmadon, he reasoned, perhaps he could learn something of the evil one's plans. Then all he would have to do is escape and inform Sensei Wu of what he had learned.

Of course, a little voice in his head said. *People escape from the Underworld every day. Piece of cake.*

There was a sudden hiss of air off to his left. Instinctively, Zane ducked. A half dozen stone daggers flew by overhead, smashing

into the opposite wall. The ninja barely had time to recover when the stairs beneath him flattened into a slide. He tumbled end over end for about one hundred yards before landing hard on a smooth platform of rock.

Zane struggled to his feet. There was darkness all around. He peered over the edges of the platform, but saw nothing. Had he skidded a little more upon landing, he would have gone over the edge and fallen to his death.

"What happened to 'no harm will come to you'?" Zane snapped. "That looks like a lot of potential harm to me."

"I had to be sure you are truly Zane, Ninja of Ice," Garmadon answered. "After all, someone might have created a . . . fake."

"For what purpose?"

"Who knows?" said Garmadon. "Why do people hide Golden Weapons that might otherwise benefit humanity? I long ago gave

up trying to determine the motivations of others."

The platform began to descend. Zane noticed the temperature falling, not nearly enough to be uncomfortable yet, but it was definitely getting colder.

"How far down am I going?" he asked.

"If it's up to me," answered Garmadon, "**all the way**."

✳ ✳ ✳

The platform finally came to a stop after what felt like a very long time. The temperature was easily below zero here, and Zane doubted this was the lowest level of the Underworld. *So I still have something to look forward to,* he thought.

It was dark, darker than any place Zane had been. Shadows skittered along the walls, moving like rodents but much too large to be any rat Zane had ever seen. Other than his own breathing, there was no sound. That was perhaps the biggest surprise. Zane had

expected to hear the sound of marching **skeleton warriors**.

"I gave them the day off," Garmadon answered, as if he had read the ninja's mind. "I wanted us to have time to talk."

"About what?"

"About you."

"Thanks," said Zane curtly. "But I'm shy. I prefer not to talk about myself."

"Then I will carry the conversation," said Garmadon. "We can talk about your skill as a ninja . . . your mission . . . your new friends . . . or perhaps you would rather talk about . . . your parents?"

CHAPTER 4

Zane's eyes narrowed. "My parents? What trick are you trying to pull?"

"No trick," Garmadon replied. "Come now, Zane, I have been trapped down here for . . . oh, a long time now. It is not, as you can see, a place bursting at the seams with entertainment opportunities. What else is there to do but observe the surface world? I have followed the course of many, many lives up there over the centuries, yours included."

Zane was intrigued. He hated feeling that way—he knew this had to be some ploy of Garmadon's—but he couldn't help wanting to

hear more. "So you're saying—" he began.

"That I know all about your past," Garmadon said. "Who you are, where you come from, why you left . . . I have all the answers, and they are yours for the asking."

"I . . . see," said Zane. "You're being very generous."

Garmadon laughed. It was a foul sound. "I don't believe I know that word. Of course, I want something in return. I am going to escape this place, Zane, no matter how my hated brother may try to prevent it. When I do, I will need warriors by my side—*competent* warriors, not Samukai's bumblers. I want you, Zane, to lead my ninja."

"Your ninja?" asked Zane. "What ninja?"

The terrible answer came in an instant. Shadows detached themselves from the walls, shadows in the shape of **ninja warriors**. As they advanced on Zane, he could see that each carried a sword of pure darkness. Soon he was

surrounded by at least a dozen spectral fighters.

Zane braced himself for a fight, at the same time reaching down into himself to find a center of inner calm. There was no room for fear in the upcoming struggle. He had to analyze his opponents rationally and find their weaknesses.

The first few shadow ninja moved in. Zane immediately saw that their fighting styles were clumsy imitations of Kai and Jay. Their blows had power behind them, but no artistry. Zane parried them easily. More joined the fight, this time imitating the moves of Cole, the ninja team leader. Again, Zane easily fended them off, though the sheer number of opponents was beginning to tax him.

The last group charged now. These were shadowy versions of Sensei Wu himself, and they were far better fighters. For the first time, Zane had to put real effort into protecting himself, which left him wide open to blows

from the other shadows. Too much more of this, and he would go down in defeat.

The time had come. Drawing on all his will-power, Zane began to spin in place. Soon, he was a **whirlwind**, unleashing the power of Spinjitzu against his foes. The shadows did not fall before his attack. Rather, Zane's cyclone shattered them into fragments of darkness that flew around the chamber.

When the last of the enemies had vanished, Zane slowed down and came to a halt. He had won. But was the battle over, or would Garmadon now unleash more ninja on him? There were plenty of shadows here to draw them from. Zane had a realistic sense of his own abilities. He knew he could not survive too many more fights like that.

"As you can see," said Garmadon, "my ninja need a little work."

"It seems they'll do, for now," said Zane,

trying to catch his breath. "But it's lucky for you Kai isn't here."

"So you can see why I need a youth of your skill to train and lead my warriors," said Garmadon. "And in exchange, you get the answers to every question that has plagued you—a more than fair trade, in my opinion."

"Speaking of opinions," Zane laughed, "yours must not be very high of me, if you think I would ever accept such an offer. I know all about you, Garmadon—your ambition, your hunger for power, your plans to dominate Ninjago. I would *never* help you. **Never.**"

Garmadon's voice grew very low, its tone betraying the anger he felt at Zane's words. "You know only what my brother wishes for you to know. As someone or other once said, 'my enemy has written all the books.'"

"Meaning?"

"Meaning there are two sides to every

story," Garmadon replied. "Do you have the courage to hear mine?"

Zane didn't know what to say. He didn't trust Garmadon at all. Sensei Wu had told him and the others more than once what a liar his brother could be. Yet part of the quest for justice was learning all the facts about a situation, rather than allowing your own prejudices to determine your actions. Could he truly be sure there was no more to the story of Wu and Garmadon than what he had been told?

"Go ahead," Zane said finally. "Tell your tale."

CHAPTER 5

The air in front of Zane began to whirl. Colors bled into one another in a giant kaleidoscope, and then a picture began to form in midair. Zane saw a much younger Sensei Wu and someone he assumed was Garmadon. There was a tall, shadowy figure standing before the brothers. Zane got an unmistakable sense that this was a man of power.

"My father," said Garmadon softly. "He created this world, did you know that? I never understood why. With two sons to look after, he chose to take on the responsibility of millions more. I suppose whatever need he

had for . . . respect? worship? . . . wasn't fully satisfied by Wu and me."

Now the figure was lifting a cloth from a table to reveal the Four Weapons of Spinjitzu. The Scythe of Quakes, Nunchuks of Lightning, Dragon Sword of Fire, and Shurikens of Ice were incredibly **powerful artifacts**. It was said that their energies were so great that no one could control all four at once. It was to protect these Weapons from Garmadon that Sensei Wu had assembled Zane and his fellow ninja. Up to now, they had been in a race against the skeleton warriors with whom Garmadon was allied to retrieve the Weapons and keep them safe.

"My father's gift to the two of us," said Garmadon. "Amazing workmanship, wouldn't you agree? He told us that when he died, the responsibility for their safekeeping would be up to us. Nothing like having something to look forward to, hmmm?"

The scene shifted again. Garmadon's father was gone now, but the Weapons remained. Sensei Wu and Garmadon were preparing them for transport.

"Sending the Weapons off to a place of concealment was actually Wu's idea," said Garmadon. "He always did like playing **hide-and-seek**, even as a child. Of course, I always won. I found it quite simple, really."

"You excel at finding things?" asked Zane.

"Oh, no," Garmadon laughed. "I excel at manipulating my brother. You see, he would hide. I would seek. After a short time, I would grow bored with trying to find him. So I would begin to sound panicked, as if I were afraid something might have happened to him. It was no longer about the game . . . it was now about Wu's safety, you see. My tenderhearted brother would feel guilty that I was so worried and would reveal himself . . . and so I won again."

"I think he knows you a little better now," said Zane.

"He certainly thinks he does," Garmadon countered. "But millennia trapped in the Underworld can change a person. Wu really has no idea what I am capable of . . . **do you**?"

"I am sure I will find out," Zane replied, "if you do not bore me to death first."

The colors swirled once more and now Zane was seeing Garmadon attempting to steal the Golden Weapons. Wu suddenly appeared, pointing an accusing finger at his brother. The image froze on that moment.

"And there we have it," said Garmadon. "That was the turning point. That is the single moment that defines me in my brother's eyes. Anything and everything else we had shared in the past was **forgotten** right then."

"You were trying to steal the Weapons!" Zane said, his voice echoing off unseen

walls. "Of course Sensei Wu turned on you. What did you think he would do?"

"Honestly?" Garmadon answered. "I thought he was asleep. I thought I would be long gone with the Four Weapons before he ever realized they were missing. And then we would play hide-and-seek again . . . by my rules."

"But it didn't work out that way," said Zane. As he talked, his eyes darted about, looking for something that might be a control panel for the platform. It was all very interesting hearing about Garmadon's youth, but there was still the little matter of escaping from this place to think about. Unfortunately, he couldn't see anything but shadows and stone.

"No. It did not, much to the misfortune of Ninjago," said Garmadon. "Think about it, Zane. Those Weapons could have been — and still might be — used to vanquish terrible evils that plague your planet. Instead, Wu chose to hide them away. When I wanted to put them to use, I was condemned as

evil and **banished** here."

"You wanted to use them for conquest and destruction," spat Zane.

"According to Wu," Garmadon shot back. "Suppose, just suppose, he has a reason to not be completely honest with you and your friends. Suppose, for all his sterling reputation, my brother is afraid to use those Weapons? That is the truth. He is afraid to do what is necessary to protect this world from evil."

Zane was not known for his sense of humor, but even he almost laughed at that. Sensei Wu had devoted his entire life to battling the forces of darkness. Now Garmadon—a shadow allied with an army of skeletons—was trying to act as if he were the true crusader for justice.

"Whose life have the Weapons improved? No one's," Garmadon continued. "What villain have they defeated? What problem have they solved? None. They have been hidden away, gathering dust, of use to no one. Is that

why they were created? I say **no**."

Zane had had enough. "And who is the judge of how they should be used? You? Samukai? One of the skeleton warriors who attacked my village?"

This time, the answer did not come from Garmadon. Instead, the scene shifted to show a kindly-looking man with a little boy sitting on his lap. The man was saying, "When you grow up, you will be very wise and very strong. I am sure of it. You must always remember that your wisdom and strength — indeed, any power you may someday have — should be used for good. To do any less would be to prove yourself unworthy of that power, Zane."

Suddenly Zane, the Ninja of Ice, who could meditate in a freezing lake without discomfort — felt terribly cold. "Who — who is that?"

"I promised you information — consider this a sign of my good faith," Garmadon answered. "That, Zane, is your father."

CHAPTER 6

Zane stood and stared for a very long time. It had to be true. The boy did look like him, and he could see an aged version of his own features on the face of his . . . father?

Father.

The word sounded strange, even rolling around in his brain. He knew it would sound even stranger if he tried to say it out loud. He reached out to touch the image, but his hand passed right through it as if it were a ghost.

"My . . ." Zane couldn't bring himself to say the word. "This man . . . where is he? Who is he?"

"Ah-ah," said Garmadon. "As I made him appear . . ." The image abruptly vanished. "So can I make him disappear. Consider this a glimpse of the treasure trove of information that waits for you here. All you have to do is say yes."

Zane stared at the empty space where his father's image had been. "Yes . . . to what?"

"Well, I am not asking you stab your friends in the back," Garmadon answered, "though that certainly would be amusing. Just slow them down a bit, here and there. You can manage that. And when the time comes, choose the winning side in the fight."

"You're asking me to be a **traitor**!"

"That's such an ugly word," said Garmadon. "I am asking you to be . . . practical. If the choice is certain victory plus a head full of knowledge about your past or sure death in battle with my skeletons, the realistic man would find the decision an easy one."

Zane shook his head. He was actually

considering Garmadon's offer, and he hated himself for it. Would this be what his father wanted? How could he someday look the man in the face if he had bought the chance to meet him with the lives of his friends?

Yet if he said no, **then what**? He would never find his father, or mother, or home. He would spend the rest of his life an empty shell, without a past. Maybe he could help Garmadon only a little, not enough to really cause a problem, and learn at least some of what he needed to know.

"Three ... two ... one," Garmadon counted down. "Time's up."

There was a flash of light. Zane blinked to clear his vision. When he could see, he found himself out of the Underworld. He was back at the edge of the pond. Had it all been a dream? No, it couldn't have been, he decided. He never had dreams like that.

Any doubts were resolved when he saw a shadow shift beneath a tree, and heard

the voice of Garmadon saying, "If we have a bargain, Zane, you will know what to do and when to do it. If you should need more convincing . . ."

The waters of the pond stirred. In their depths, Zane could see his father with an elderly woman. They were sitting in a farmhouse with a picture of Zane on the table before them. The woman—his mother?—was crying softly. Then the image was gone as swiftly as it had appeared.

CHAPTER 7

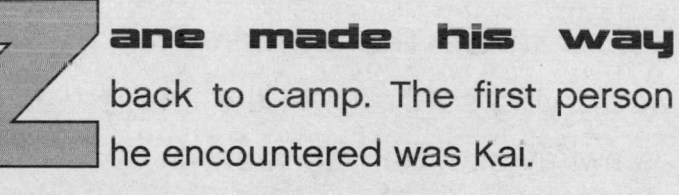**ane made his way** back to camp. The first person he encountered was Kai.

"Hey, are you all right?" the Ninja of Fire asked. "You look like you've seen a ghost."

"Or two," Zane replied softly.

"Huh?"

"Never mind. Where is Sensei Wu?"

Kai pointed toward the center of camp. Sensei Wu was sitting by the campfire, staring pensively into the flames. Zane walked over and sat down next to him. At first, the sensei did not seem to even notice his presence. But after a few moments, Wu said, "The

birds of worry nest in your hair, Zane. Do you wish to tell me why?"

Zane hesitated. Did he really want to say, *Well, I was considering betraying you for my own selfish reasons?* No, it was best not to.

"No, Sensei," he answered.

Wu nodded. "Do you believe your doubts and fears threaten our mission?"

"I don't know," answered Zane.

The sensei sipped from a cup of tea that seemed to appear as if by magic in his hand. Zane would have sworn it had not been there moments before. "There was once a **golden dragon fish**," the aged warrior began. "It lived among a very great school of its brothers. One day, the fish broke away from the school seeking adventure, and met a shark. The shark invited the little fish to travel with him and feed off the mites that collected on his scales. Soon, the dragon fish fell into the way of life of traveling with the shark. Its

success was linked to that of the great predator.

"Months later, the shark spotted a school of fish and went on the hunt. To his dismay, the dragon fish saw that the prey fish the shark was after were his brothers. He had time to warn them—but doing so would mean the end of his pleasant life with the shark . . . decisions, decisions."

Does he know? wondered Zane. *Or only suspect? I must be careful.*

"Well, questions of loyalty are always difficult ones," said the Ninja of Ice. "It is not always easy to know which side to be on, or what to believe."

"Believe in yourself," the sensei said. "Be true to what you believe, to your ideals, and you will find your choice has been made for you."

"Thank you, Sensei," said Zane. "I believe I understand. By the way . . . what happened to the dragon fish?"

"Oh, he fled the shark and warned his brothers."

"That is commendable," said Zane. "His loyalty to his school was more important to him than his own interests. He must have been very proud of himself for making such a choice."

"Indeed, he was," the sensei replied, "right up to the moment that the shark ate him."

Zane **shuddered**.

Cole approached, carrying the golden Scythe of Quakes, one of the Four Weapons of Spinjitzu. Like Zane, Cole was a pretty serious sort. He took being field leader of the ninja team very seriously. "Are you ready, Zane?" he asked.

"Ready for what?"

"I have not yet told him," Sensei Wu said to Cole. Turning to Zane, he extended his hand. In his palm were the Shurikens of Ice, yet another of the valuable artifacts. "You and Cole have found your Golden Weapons. The

time may come when you are forced to use them. I want you to go some distance from camp and train with them."

"Wait," said Zane, confused. "When we found the Scythe, you told us we must not ever use it. Isn't it dangerous to practice fighting with these Weapons?"

Sensei Wu nodded. "Times change. The wise man changes with them. We have retrieved two of the four Weapons, and my brother, Garmadon, will be growing desperate. **Anything** may happen now."

Zane barely heard his answer. All he could think of was what would happen if he gave the two Golden Weapons to Garmadon. Would that be enough to buy information about his past?

It wouldn't be so bad, would it? he asked himself. *As long as we get the Dragon Sword of Fire and the Nunchuks of Lightning, we can stop Garmadon. It would simply be a stalemate.*

"Let's go," said Cole. "We don't have much time."

"No," Zane replied. "I guess we don't."

Zane took the Shurikens. Something felt wrong about all this, but the image in his mind of his parents drove all other thoughts away. He rose in silence and followed Cole out of the camp.

CHAPTER 8

They stopped walking when they reached an empty area. It wasn't far from the cave where Zane had found Garmadon. If Zane had believed in fate, he would have surely seen this as a sign.

Cole was twirling the Scythe, being careful not to strike anything and unleash the Weapon's seismic power. Soon, he was moving so fast that the Scythe was just a golden blur.

"Get started," Cole ordered. "Try getting the feel of the weight and balance of the Shuriken. That will help you master throwing it."

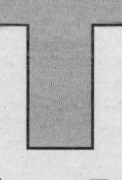

Zane did as he was told. That feeling that something was wrong kept nagging at him. What was it—something about the Shuriken itself, perhaps? He had held it only briefly when the team had retrieved it from the Ice Fortress. What could have happened between then and now? And was there more to the sensei's decision to allow training with the Golden Weapons than the old man was letting on?

Something whistled through the air past Zane's head. An instant later, Cole hit the ground, unconscious. Zane rushed over to him. He had been struck by a thrown rock. There was a big lump on his head, but the ninja team leader was alive.

A half dozen skeleton warriors stepped out of the surrounding woods, followed by another skeleton, this one with four arms. The Ninja of Ice immediately recognized this new arrival, and knew he was in **serious trouble**.

"Samukai," breathed Zane.

The empty eye sockets of the ruler of the Underworld narrowed. "You flesh-covered types all look alike to me," Samukai rasped. "But I remember you. You're the one with no past. Well, I have news for you: You have no future, either."

Zane glanced from Samukai to Cole, then back again. It was time to make his choice. He took a step away from his fallen friend and raised the Shuriken, as if preparing to throw it. Samukai moved back a little, but none of the other skeletons did. The four-armed warrior knew the legendary power of the Shurikens of Ice: Obviously, his soldiers had no clue what they faced.

A moment passed, then two. Combat or surrender? Loyalty to his team or betrayal on behalf of a life he could not remember? Which would it be? As he turned the Shuriken over and over in his fingers, he felt that sense of wrongness yet again. But this

time he knew its cause . . . and he knew what he had to do.

Zane lowered his arm and extended the Shurikens toward Samukai. "Here. Take them. The Scythe, too — your master knows my price."

Samukai didn't move. His expression was wary. He had not become ruler of the massive Underworld by rushing into traps, and that was what this felt like.

"Who do you think you are trying to deceive, child?" said Samukai. "Some minor shade on his first visit back to Ninjago? One of my idiotic soldiers? Do you expect me to believe you are going to simply hand over two of the Four Weapons of Spinjitzu without a **fight**?"

"Believe it or not," answered Zane. "You have thirty seconds to accept my offer. After that, you can try to take them, but I do not like your chances. Or you can go back to Garmadon and tell him you had the chance

at half of his desired treasure and you turned it down."

Samukai did some quick mental calculations. Garmadon was not his master, despite what this sniveling human thought, but Sensei Wu's dark brother was a powerful ally just the same. It was doubtful Garmadon would take kindly to finding out the Shurikens and Scythe could have been had and were allowed to slip away.

Shoving one of his skeleton warriors toward Zane, Samukai said, "Give the Weapons to this one. He is too slow to know what to do with them, so there is no risk of betrayal. You said Garmadon would know your price — I would like to know it, too. I do not like to 'purchase' items without knowing the terms of sale."

The skeleton approached. Zane handed him the Shurikens, then bent down to pick up the Scythe of Quakes. He gave that to the skeleton as well, saying, "Be careful with these. Dropping them would be . . . bad."

"Answer my question!" snapped Samukai.

"That *is* my price," Zane replied, "the answers to questions."

Samukai took the two Golden Weapons from his warrior. A smile appeared like a crack in his skull. "Do you want us to **strike you down** now? You know, so that you can tell Sensei Wu you were attacked, defeated, and the Weapons stolen from you? I am sure we can make your battle damage look most convincing."

"No, thanks," said Zane. "Just give me what I asked for."

Samukai cocked his head and paused, as if listening to something no one else could hear. Then he said, "Garmadon says, return to the cave. You'll get what you need there."

"What about my friend here?"

Samukai shrugged. "If we wanted him dead, we would have thrown a **bigger rock**."

Zane couldn't argue with that logic,

twisted though it might be. He backed away from the skeletons, keeping an eye on them until they had all withdrawn into the woods. Cole was already beginning to stir. Zane turned and headed for the cave, hoping he would make it inside before his friend spotted him. He didn't want Cole placed in any more danger because of him. What he had to do now, he had to do alone.

CHAPTER 9

The cavern was still pitch-black inside, but now the darkness seemed alive with movement. More of Garmadon's shadow ninja, perhaps? Zane stood still, waiting for the platform to descend and take him to the world below. But nothing happened. His host, it seemed, saw no reason to continue the tour of the Underworld.

"An impressive beginning," said Garmadon, his voice slithering out from all corners of the cave. "I chose wisely, I see."

"Not a beginning," Zane corrected, "an

ending. Give me the information you promised and our deal is done."

"Do you think it is that easy?"

Zane stood his ground and said firmly, "I know it is. I have lived with my mysteries for a long time now and could keep doing it, if necessary. You have spent far longer trapped in the Underworld and cannot stand it. Seems to me that you need me more than I need you."

Garmadon gave a soft chuckle. "Very well, then. A bargain is a bargain. Look, Zane."

Once again, the portal appeared in mid-air. This time, Zane saw himself as a small child with his father and mother. Their home was a small shack in what appeared to be a little village. Zane was sitting on the lawn, playing with a stick, while his father chopped wood and his mother hung up washing.

"Your father was a woodworker," Garmadon said. "He carved wood into axe

handles, toys, plates, bowls, utensils, all sorts of boring things like that. Your mother was a seamstress, sewing new clothes and repairing old ones for others. Between the two of them, they made enough money to keep a little food on the table and take care of their young son."

The scene shifted. Now a much older Zane was walking down a road. It must have been just past sunset, for the road was very dark. All at once, a horse-drawn cart came **thundering** around a curve, dangerously fast. It struck Zane a glancing blow and the young man fell unconscious in the road.

"You were on your way to purchase some supplies from a neighboring town," Garmadon continued. "The driver of the cart never even saw you. The next morning, you awoke in the road with no memory of what had happened. End of story."

"What?" said Zane. "What about my parents? Are they still alive? What village are they from?"

"If you want more, you must do more for me," Garmadon replied.

Zane shook his head. "No. Never."

"Then I have half of the Four Weapons, and you have half the story, and that is how it is," said Garmadon. "It cost you the trust of your friends, your honor, and your pride. It cost me . . . hmmm . . . the hour or so I needed to make up that story."

At first, Zane felt like crying out in anger. Everything Garmadon had told him about his past—it had all been a lie. His parents, his home, all of it, nothing more than a trick to get him to betray Sensei Wu. Yet instead of raging at Garmadon, Zane actually smiled.

This seemed to annoy Garmadon. "What are you smiling about?" he demanded.

"Oh, I was just thinking about bargains,"

Zane answered. "You do get what you pay for, don't you? You gave me a phony past . . . and I gave you phony Weapons of Spinjitzu."

"What?!?" roared Garmadon, loud enough to shake the cavern.

"I can't take the credit," Zane explained. "Your brother must have sensed what you were up to. He gave Cole and me fake versions of our Golden Weapons, suspecting they might wind up in your hands. I didn't know, at first. But when I got ready to throw the Shurikens of Ice at Samukai, I realized they were too light. True gold is very heavy, and this felt more like iron, painted gold."

Zane turned and started walking out of the cave. "I am afraid, Garmadon, you traded a lie for a lie. Our business today has ended."

Three skeletons appeared in the mouth of the cave. Behind him, Zane could feel the shadows taking form as ninja. He was surrounded.

"It is ended when I say it is ended,"

Garmadon snarled. "No one makes a fool out of me."

There was a blur of movement at the entrance to the cave. Something **smashed** into the three skeletons, bowling them over. An instant later, Cole stood alone in their place.

"No one has to, Garmadon," Cole said. "You do such a good job of it by yourself."

The shadow ninja charged. Zane dove forward, landing on his hands, and lashed back with both feet. His kicks staggered two of the ninja. Before the rest could close in, he rolled into a somersault and sprang to his feet next to Cole.

"How did you find me?" asked Zane.

"I saw that rock coming a mile away," Cole replied. "It grazed me . . . well, maybe a little more than that . . . but I was awake the whole time. I would have shown up sooner, but I had to see what you would do."

The shadow ninja rushed out of the

cave. This time, their movements were more fluid, their blows harder, and their imitations of the young ninja more accurate. But this time, Zane was not facing them alone. He and Cole worked like a perfect team, ducking and dodging and then **striking hard**. Cole confused a foe by dropping to his back and then landing a kick in the shadow ninja's midsection, sending him flying through the air. Zane saw a shadowy being coming and leaped high, coming down with a two-fisted slam that smashed the dark ninja into the ground.

After a short but furious battle, the shadow ninja started retreating into the cave. Zane started in after them, but was brought up short by Cole. "No, let them go. We need to get back to the sensei."

"But—"

"Come on. It's over, for now. There will be another day, I promise you."

CHAPTER 10

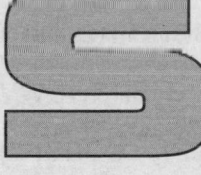 ensei Wu was waiting when they got back to camp. He motioned for Zane to join him by the fire. "You guessed that the Weapons were fake, and so you gave them to the enemy."

Zane nodded.

"And if you hadn't known they were frauds? Would you still have handed them over to Samukai? You feel you are not sure of the answer to that question, and it bothers you, does it not?"

Again, Zane nodded, his eyes on the ground.

"Fortunately for us both, I do know the answer," Sensei Wu said, smiling. "I may not know your origins, but I am certain of what is in your heart. Just like the dragon fish, when the time came to make a choice, you would do what is right . . . even if it cost you your life. That is why I chose you. That is why you said yes."

"Thank you, Sensei," said Zane quietly. "But I wonder . . . will I ever know about my past? Will I ever meet my parents?"

"I truly hope so," the sensei replied. "And when you do, tell them the tale of this day . . . tell them how you did their memory honor, even when that memory was lost to you."

Cole walked up to the fire. "Sensei, you said we need to get moving. I have the others packed up and ready."

"Yes, indeed," the sensei said, getting to his feet. "We have a third Weapon to find, but it is not a long journey. Just to the **edge of the world** and

beyond. There are more mysteries to be explored, my young ninja . . . and, perhaps, some answers to be found along the way."

CALLING ALL NINJA!
GET THESE LEGO® NINJAGO BOOKS!

INCLUDES YOUR VERY OWN LEGO® MINIFIGURE!

INCLUDES OVER 100 STICKERS OF NINJAGO HEROES, VILLAINS, VEHICLES, AND MORE!

SCHOLASTIC

www.scholastic.com
www.ninjago.com

NINJA11